Tonka®

FIRE TRUCK TO THE RESCUE

Tonka®

FIRE TRUCK TO THE RESCUE

Written by Ann Martin
Illustrated by Steven James Petruccio

SCHOLASTIC INC.
New York Toronto London Auckland Sydney

Look for these other books about Tonka trucks:

Working Hard with the Mighty Dump Truck
Working Hard with the Busy Fire Truck
Working Hard with the Mighty Loader
Working Hard with the Mighty Mixer

ISBN 0-590-48854-6

12 11 10 9 8 7 6 5 4 3 2 1 4 5 6 7 8 9/9

Printed in the U.S.A. 24

First Scholastic printing, October 1994

One afternoon Eric and his sister, Amanda, were playing in their front yard when they heard *Whoo! Whoo! Whoo!* and *Clang! Clang! Clang!* They looked around and saw a big, red fire truck racing down their street.

"There must be a fire on our street," they said.

They ran to the curb just in time to watch the big, red fire truck whiz by. It stopped at the house where Mrs. Brown lives alone with her cat.

Eric ran into his house to ask his mom if they could watch the firefighters put out the fire. His mom said, "Just a minute, I'll go with you." And she went to get her coat.

The three of them ran down the street to Mrs. Brown's house and joined the other neighbors who were standing in front of the fire truck. The fire truck was as long as two houses.

The fire chief was giving orders to the firefighters as they were jumping out of the fire truck.

One of the firefighters was out on the street making sure the people who had come to see the fire did not get in the way.

Two firefighters ran to the front door and banged on it. When there was no answer they started breaking down the door with an ax and ran inside.

Eric saw flames and smoke coming out of the upstairs windows.

A firefighter was climbing a ladder that came up from the fire truck right to the second-floor window.

Another firefighter was busy attaching the long fire hose to the hydrant. Now the firefighter on the ladder was able to squirt a huge gush of water through the window where the flames were coming out.

A police car and an ambulance with their sirens blaring and red lights flashing were speeding toward Mrs. Brown's house.

Eric saw Mrs. Brown come around from the back of the house with a firefighter helping her by the arm. She seemed to be fine, just a little bit shaken up. She came over to stand with the rest of the neighbors. Eric's mom went over to her.

Mrs. Brown was very relieved to be out of the house. "The firefighters were great," she said. "And they are going back in to rescue my cat, Muffin."

The smoke began to clear and no more flames were coming from the house.

Eric waited nervously to see if Muffin was okay. At last one of the firefighters came out holding the white cat.

It seemed that the fire was over. The rest of the firefighters began coming out of the house

While they put away their equipment on the fire truck, the chief went back into the house to make sure the fire was really out and there was no more danger.

The fire chief came out and said that there wasn't too much damage, just a lot of water inside the house.

Eric asked lots of questions about the fire and the truck and all the equipment the firefighters used.

The fire chief said that all the firefighters were tired from putting out the fire, but he invited Eric and his sister and his mom to come to the firehouse for a tour.

The next day, they drove to the firehouse. The fire chief greeted them at the door.

Inside was a big, red fire truck.

The chief said, "The fire truck holds the equipment we need to put out fires. Why don't you climb up here where the firefighters stand when they ride to a fire?"

Eric and Amanda climbed up. The fire chief pointed out the hose that was all rolled up. It was taller than Eric. The fire chief said, "When this is unrolled, it is longer than the street you live on."

The fire chief explained that when the hose is hooked up to a fire hydrant, the firefighter can spray water from a nozzle on top of the ladder.

Eric said, “Up close the ladder seems really big.”

“And it gets even bigger when we need to get into high windows,” the chief said. He explained how the ladder extends way up high right from the truck.

As they stepped off the truck, Eric saw the firefighters' uniforms hanging against the wall.

The chief said, "The firefighters' clothes are called turnout gear. Everything is fireproof. There are coats and gloves, rubber pants and boots. The firefighters also wear special hats called helmets."

The chief let Eric and Amanda try on some helmets. He told them they could wear the helmets around the station if they wanted to. They were a lot heavier than they looked.

The fire chief told them how important it is to keep the fire truck clean and shiny.

Then he showed them the pole that the firefighters slide down when it is time to go put out a fire.

As he led Eric and Amanda upstairs, he explained that the firehouse is more than just a place to park the fire truck. “It’s also like another home for the firefighters. Since we have to be available all the time in case of a fire, we work day and night. Sometimes we sleep here on cots.”

He showed them the living area where the firefighters relax when there are no fires to put out.

Eric saw a big, white dog with black spots sleeping in the corner by a chair. “This is our firehouse dog,” the chief said. “His name is Sparky and everyone loves him as if he were their own dog.”

Eric and Amanda petted Sparky and he wagged his tail at them.

Next the chief showed them the kitchen and dining room where the firefighters take turns preparing and serving meals.

Suddenly Eric, Amanda, and their mom jumped when they heard the loud *Clang! Clang! Clang!* of the alarm bell.

The fire chief sprang into action along with all the other firefighters in the firehouse.

They stopped whatever they were doing and ran to the fire pole, taking turns sliding down.

By the time Eric, Amanda, and their mom got down the stairs, most of the firefighters had already put on their gear and were climbing onto the big, red fire truck.

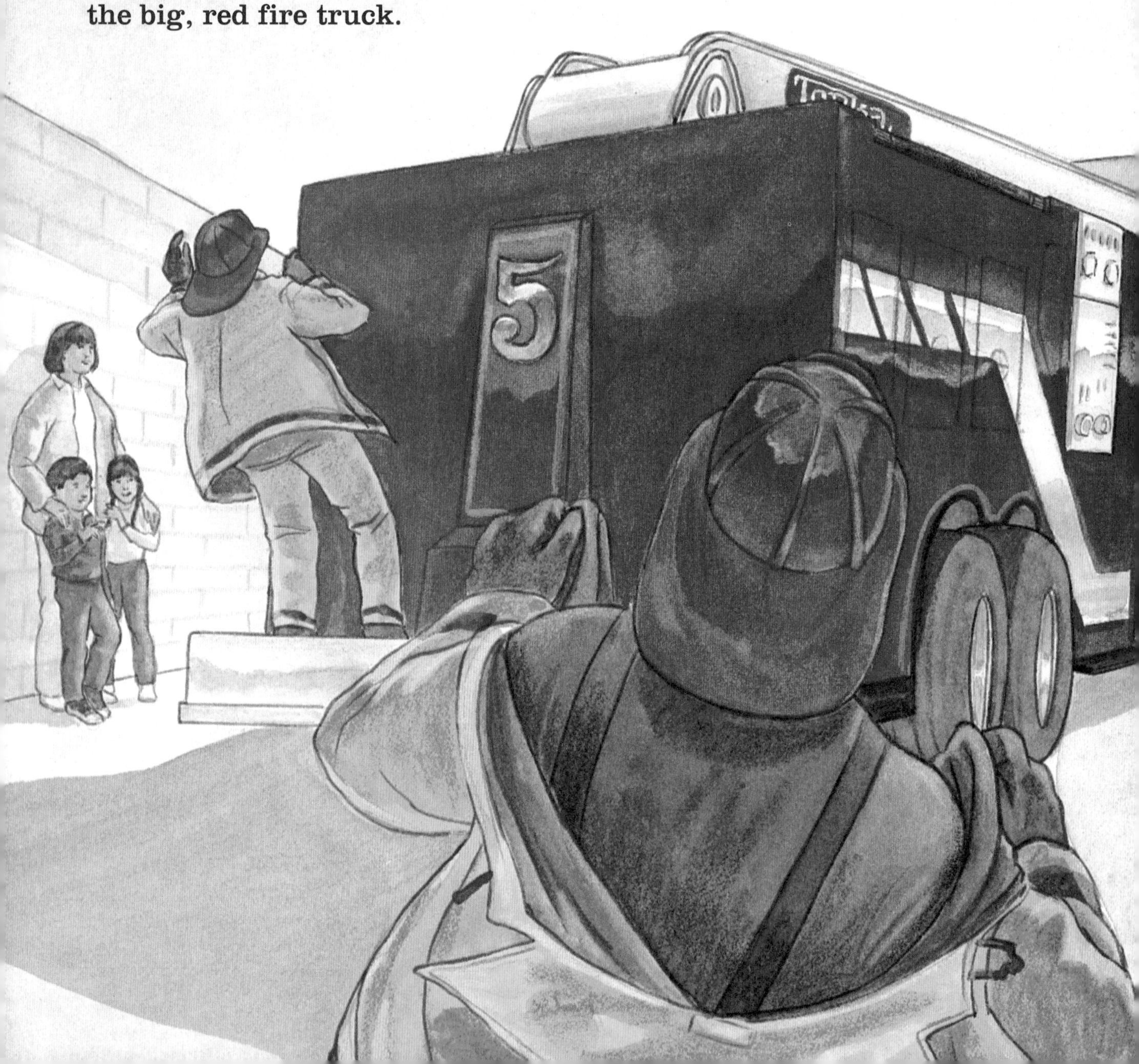

Eric, Amanda, and their mom waved good-bye as the big, red fire truck and the brave firefighters left the firehouse to put out another fire.